THE
HISTORY
CHANNEL
PRESENTS

BY CAMERON BANKS

BIZARRE BEINGS

SCHOLASTIC INC.
New York   Toronto   London   Auckland   Sydney
Mexico City   New Delhi   Hong Kong   Buenos Aires

No part of this publication may be reproduced in whole or in part, stored in a retrieval system, or transmitted in any form or by any means, electronic, mechanical, photocopying, recording, or otherwise, without written permission of the publisher.
For information regarding permission, write to Scholastic Inc., Attention: Permissions Department, 557 Broadway, New York, NY 10012.

ISBN 0-439-40149-6

Book design by Louise Bova

12 11 10 9 8 7 6 5 4 3 2 1   2 3 4 5 6 7/0
Printed in the U.S.A.
First Scholastic printing, September 2002

CONTENTS

CREEPY!

They lurk in the world's deep waters, lie atop mountain peaks, and tell incredible tales from a dark and distant past. They appear everywhere, from the deserts of Africa to the lakes of Europe. They're as down-to-earth as our own ancestors and as high-flying as our imaginations. Who are they? The most bizarre beings in the world, of course! These curious creatures have fascinated, mystified, and even scared people for ages.

If you'd like to meet some of the world's creepiest creatures yourself, you've come to the right place! With this book, you can travel through time and space without ever leaving your own home. You'll discover the select few beings that qualify for the title of Most Bizarre! And you'll have the opportunity to decide for yourself whether some of these creatures are real . . . or too strange to be believed!

Working with The History Channel, *Bizarre Beings* has found the stories behind some of the most amazing creatures *ever*. And whether you're a believer or not, one thing is certain: After meeting these creatures, you'll never look at something as "strange" in the same way again. Once you know what you're looking for, maybe someday you'll discover a *bizarre being* of your very own!

CHILLIN' WITH THE CAVEMEN

A group of amazing beings survived for 100,000 years . . . then mysteriously died out! Neandertals living 50,000 years ago were three times as strong as modern man, but were they the fierce, stupid creatures of "cavemen" cartoons? Read on to find out!

INTRODUCING . . . THE NEANDERTALS!

Who were the Neandertals? We know that they wore animal skins, lived in packs, were much stronger than Arnold Schwarzenegger, and hunted wild creatures like woolly mammoths for food. Most lived in caves so we have come to call them cavemen. The Neandertals were different from modern-day humans in many, many ways. They were much more muscular and much stronger, for one, and they also had different-shaped faces and bodies. Plus, the food they ate was different from the kind we eat. These cavemen didn't have school, electricity, or even real houses! Still, you'll be surprised to know that you're actually *related* to these bizarre beings.

Neandertals were the result of a natural process called evolution. Evolution is the theory that all species of plants and animals developed from earlier forms of living things. And evolution is the process through which plants and animals — from trees to humans — change and develop! This process takes millions of years, and there are many steps along the way.

Anthropologists and other scientists agree that Neandertals fall somewhere between the first humans and modern man! They lived for more than 100,000 years. But scientists don't agree on what

CREATURE FEATURE

Did you know that Neandertal's name has been spelled and pronounced in *many* different ways over the years? (For one, it was once spelled "Neanderthal" — with an *h*.) Most people agree on the current spelling — with no *h*!

happened to the Neandertals. Why did they disappear?

Meet the fascinating family called Neandertal — your distant relatives! We'll find out how they lived and perhaps . . . why they died.

FIRST FINDINGS

Scientists believe our earliest ancestors appeared in Africa and migrated to Asia and Europe. Neandertals were named after Germany's Neander Valley, where fossils of a new kind of caveman were first found in 1856. Since then, scientists have found the bones of more than 1,000 Neandertals — more than any other species of early human!

These bones tell the story of what Neandertals looked like. They had two arms and two legs like modern humans, but they were much shorter. Most adult Neandertals weren't much more than five feet tall. They were muscular, however, with stocky and powerful bodies. They were very strong.

"The general level of their

5

strength [was] in their arms and shoulders," says caveman expert Erik Trinkhaus. This expert also estimated that cavemen were about "two or three times" as strong as the average modern-day human. In an arm-wrestling contest between you and a Neandertal, let's just say the Neandertal would win . . . hands down!

FACE FACTS

An important difference between humans of today and Neandertals is the skull. Pretend you don't have any skin or hair for a moment. (Gross, right? But just pretend any-

MONSTER-SIZE CREATURE FEATURE

Nearly every creature has a scientific name along with the common name we use in conversation. Usually that scientific name is in Latin and tells the "family" that an animal belongs to. For example, a dog's scientific name is *Canis familiaris*. All birds are from the family *Aves* [AH-vays]. Your family has its own name, too, but you share a scientific family name with all human beings, no matter where they are from! All humans are *Homo sapiens* [HO-moh SAY-pea-ens], which means "wise being." Neandertals were called *Homo neandertalenis*.

way!) Your skull is fairly round. Your forehead is mostly up-and-down. And the bone underneath your eyebrows doesn't stick out too much.

Neandertals, on the other hand, had much flatter skulls. Their foreheads sloped from the front of their faces back toward the center of their skulls. They also had a very prominent ridge of bone above their eyes. They probably had much bigger noses than today's humans. And they didn't have very big chins. Because Neandertals lived in very *cold* climates, they all probably had a lot of hair. And inside those odd-shaped skulls were brains that sometimes were larger than our own!

KNUCKLE SCRAPERS? NOT!

Did Neandertals walk upright? Or did they amble along, stooped over and scraping their knuckles against the ground? For years, we were certain that Neandertals walked stooped over. But we were very wrong!

The problems began in 1908, when scientists discovered a com-

BIZARRO-RAMA: QUICK QUIZ

Neandertals lived through centuries of ice ages without sophisticated tools or weapons. True or false?

(Answer: True)

plete skeleton of a Neandertal man in France. Nicknamed "The Old Man from La Chapelle," the skeleton had knock-knees and a back that was very hunched over. Scientists figured that *all* Neandertals looked like this, so they created drawings of cavemen with cramped, stooped walking styles. They even said that cavemen were slow and clumsy.

But later research showed that Neandertals walked upright and were actually well-coordinated! "The Old Man from La Chapelle" was just that, an old man. He probably had arthritis, a bone disease that made it hard for him to stand up straight.

CREATURE FEATURE

In 1912, some bones were found near Piltdown, England. Scientists thought they had found the mysterious "missing link" between apes and man. However, forty years later, it was proven that the "Piltdown Man" was nothing but a bunch of human bones doctored up to look old. It is one of the most famous hoaxes in the history of science!

DAILY LIFE FOR CAVEMEN — AND CAVEWOMEN!

Neandertals left behind no writing or records of any sort. That makes it difficult for scholars and scientists to study them. Still, through years of sleuthing, scientists have been able to learn a lot about what daily life was like for people who lived during the time of the woolly mammoths and giant elephants!

CAVE HOMES: FIRE AND LICE!

In the caves where Neandertals lived, scientists have found fire pits and piles of ash, which means the cavemen had learned to use fire. This was very important because

9

BIZARRO-RAMA: QUICK QUIZ

During the time of the Neandertal, everyone lived in the open or in caves, in all sorts of weather. When hunting was finished in one area, men, women, and children had to travel together to find food, sometimes walking many miles in a day. True or false?

(Answer: True)

without fire, they might have frozen to death. Fire gave them light to see the world around them and provided them with a way to cook the animals they caught for food.

Most important, fire helped protect the Neandertals from dangerous animals. Light a fire in the mouth of a cave and no fierce creature would dare cross it to have you for dinner!

Interestingly, Neandertals used fire to clean house. The mats of grass and straw they used for bedding often got filled with lice, ticks, and other nasty insects . . . so Neandertals *burned* them! Of course, that meant that they had to get new beds afterwards, but at least the lice were gone!

WHAT'S FOR DINNER?

Neandertals were hunters who had to hunt and kill for their dinners. That often meant a fierce fight with an enormous beast like a rhino or mammoth elephant! Neandertals didn't have bows and arrows or guns to hunt. Amazingly, they used only sticks, sharp stones, and heavy rocks!

Hunting was hard and very dangerous work. Catching a big meal sometimes meant that some of the Neandertals wouldn't be around to enjoy it! After they did catch an animal, Neandertals used sharp stone tools to cut up the animal. They sometimes used their fires to cook it, but they might have eaten parts of the animal raw.

Neandertals also ate birds, plants, and small rodents (not your idea of a great meal, right?). And not a bit of the creature was ever wasted. Neandertals made coverings out of animal skins to protect themselves against cold weather. They sometimes used bones for tools as well. Pretty smart thinking for these prehistoric people!

WOMEN AND KIDS

Scientists believe that in Neandertal families it was usually the men who would leave the caves to go out and hunt for food for long periods of time. The women had to stay behind to protect the children. Neandertal women had to be just as rough and tough as the men.

Although they had to do a lot of hard work, it seems cavewomen were not treated very well by the cavemen. Based on findings, scientists believe that women were treated with less respect than men because they were not honored by being buried with tools when they died.

Children had to be very tough, too. Only the strongest kids survived. They might even have had to fight for their food! Also, as soon as they were able, boys probably joined the men out hunting. Girls became mothers at a very young age. It was a hard time to be a kid.

CREATURE FEATURE

Neandertals buried people with flints, stone tools, animal horns, and even flower petals. Some scientists think Neandertals may have even believed in an afterlife of some kind. This would explain why they felt their dead might need tools and weapons as they left this world.

A KINDER, GENTLER CAVE PEOPLE

Neandertal women and children may have had a hard time, but in some ways, the cave people were kinder and gentler than we once thought. For example, scientists used to believe that Neandertals could not — or *would not* — take care of their sick and injured relatives and friends. However, discoveries of fossils showing healed broken bones indicate that the Neandertals actually cared for the sick. A person with a broken leg wasn't much use to anyone, but instead of leaving that sick person to die, Neandertals took care of him or her.

Research shows that Neandertals probably buried their dead as well. They were among the first people *ever* to do so. In many places, scientists have found the skeletons of Neandertals carefully laid out instead of just left on the ground.

Some of the skeletons found today have ani-

BIZARRO-RAMA: QUICK QUIZ

The woolly mammoth was an ancestor of the elephant that was smaller and much hairier than its modern cousins. True or false?

(Answer: False. Woolly mammoths were much larger than modern elephants!)

CREATURE FEATURE

In some cases, dead bodies became more than something to bury for the Neandertal. If there were no animals around to eat and a Neandertal happened to pass away, he or she might soon become dinner. Sometimes becoming a *cannibal* like that was the difference between living and dying for early man.

mal horns or stone tools buried with them. One grave was found with a skeleton that had been painted with colorful plant dyes. So scientists learned that these were not just grunting cavemen. They actually cared for their dead and disposed of them properly!

DID CAVEMEN SPEAK?

No one really knows if these mysterious beings could actually ask their neighbor to pass the woolly mammoth. Did cavemen just grunt, like they do in movies? Or did they have an actual language that got lost in time?

Believe it or not, one tiny bone may hold the answer. In 1983, in a cave in Israel, the first Neandertal hyoid [HIGH-oid] bone was found. This little bone, not much bigger than your thumbnail, is located in the base of the tongue. This bone is vital for speaking. Without it, you'd be about as talkative as a fish!

The fact that Neandertals had this bone reveals that the cave people might actually have used language to communicate! Instead of grunting and growling like cavemen in movies do, Neandertals may have used words and sounds that were more complex than ever before imagined.

Somebody certainly had to be able to yell: "Watch out for that rampaging rhino!"

NEANDERTALS: WHAT HAPPENED?

After being around for about 100,000 years, Neandertals began to go into a decline . . . and eventually disappeared altogether. Why did this happen?

HERE COME THE CRO-MAGNONS!

About 40,000 years ago, another type of early human came from Africa into the lands where Neandertals lived. Their faces looked somewhat like the faces of Neandertals, but they were obviously different. These people were taller, with longer arms that were better at throwing spears.

These new kids on the block were called Cro-Magnons. Just how they lived — or fought — with the Neandertals is *still* a big debate among scientists. One theory says that there was just about enough food for Neandertals . . . and suddenly, Cro-Magnons were coming into their territory. There wasn't enough food for everyone. Something had to give!

Just what *did* give, however, might never be known. Did the two groups fight? Did they get along? Some caves have been found where these two types of prehuman creatures seemed to have lived together.

In a fight, a Neandertal would have been much stronger. But Cro-Magnons brought with them better tools and weapons.

On the other hand, Cro-Magnons and Neandertals might have just become mixed up together. They weren't that much different, after all. Did they have children together? Did they get along, with the Cro-Magnons teaching the Neandertals about tools and the Neandertals teaching the Cro-Magnons about local animals?

Some scientists think they did just that. Others believe that battles raged for control of the land. But there's one thing everyone agrees on: About 10,000 years after the Cro-Magnons showed up, suddenly, there were *no more* Neandertals!

THE MYSTERY CONTINUES

Thousands of years later, here you are, reading about your ancestors. Does a little bit of a Neandertal live in you?

As scientist Erik Trinkhaus has observed, studying the Neandertals tells us an awful lot about the power of the human mind. It shows what people can do under the most difficult conditions. Today, we can even learn a lot about ourselves by studying those who came before us.

What will happen to us? Will a group of strange new creatures like the Cro-Magnons show

CREATURE FEATURE

Cro-Magnons came from northern Africa into Europe about 50,000 years ago. They used bones, stones, and sticks to form better tools and spears. They also employed a wooden device called an atlatl that could make spears go farther. They were the first people to make art, using plant dyes to paint on cave walls. The Cro-Magnons were much more like us than Neandertals were.

up someday and make us disappear? Or will we carry on, surviving and thriving like the Neandertals did for many years? That's one mystery we can't solve right now, but maybe, someday, *you* just might.

②

MOTHER NATURE'S MUMMIES

Forget old King Tut and those amazing ancient Egyptians for a moment and consider this: From high mountaintops to murky peat bogs, from frozen landscapes to scorching deserts, *Mother Nature* makes mummies the world over.

NATURAL MUMMIES

If you've ever seen the hit *Mummy* movies, you know that people have tried to preserve dead bodies for ages! But not all mummies are wrapped up in bandages. Some bodies become mummified thanks to natural forces like heat and cold! And they've lasted a long, long time . . .

SELF-PRESERVATION?

Over the last 200 years, scientists have discovered extremely well-preserved bodies in various parts of the world. The natural processes that normally break down the body's tissue and flesh were somehow stopped — yet the bodies didn't appear to be treated with chemicals! Cold temperatures, high altitudes, very dry conditions, and even mysterious bogs have all helped create what scientists call "natural mummies."

Because mummies preserve the past, they are like messengers. They can tell us about what life was like in past times. These natural mummies also present a big mystery: How did they come to be so *perfectly* preserved?

BIZARRO-RAMA: QUICK QUIZ

Our bodies are full of bacteria with destructive enzymes that protect us from germs while we're alive. When we die, those destructive enzymes break down — and our bodies dissolve themselves! True or false?

(Answer: True . . . and gross)

OTZI THE ICEMAN

In 1991, when a landslide in the Otze Valley of the high, dry Austrian-Italian Alps exposed some hillside, something else appeared: the oldest, most dramatic natural mummy ever found! The body was small, dark, and frozen solid . . . so the

MONSTER-SIZE CREATURE FEATURE

The people of ancient Egypt created the best-known mummies *ever*. Found in huge tombs built for Egypt's dead kings, mummies are remains of real humans, carefully preserved after death by special chemicals and wrappings. Ancient Egyptians believed they could live on in an afterlife by preserving their bodies.

The Egyptians removed organs and filled what was left of the body with special oils and liquids that kept it from dissolving. They then wrapped the bodies in linen cloth and placed them into airtight tombs that also helped preserve the bodies from the effects of burial and erosion. Impressive, right? Still, the Egyptians were *ages* behind *Mother Nature* in preserving bodies. . . .

specimen became known as the Iceman! The discovery of the Iceman (nicknamed "Otzi" after the valley where the mummy was found) thrilled scientists — and the world. Otzi appeared on magazine covers and television shows *everywhere.*

BIZARRO-RAMA: QUICK QUIZ

Otzi is the oldest mummy *of any kind* ever found. True or false?

(Answer: False. A large bison nick-named Blue Babe was found in Alaska in 1979. Blue Babe had been on ice for 36,000 years!)

THE AMAZINGLY ADVANCED OTZI!

At first, scientists believed Otzi died in about 2500 B.C.E., near the beginning of what is called the Copper Age, because of objects found with the mummy. (Otzi's "gear" included an ax with a blade made of copper.) But radiocarbon dating, which tests the age of tissue and other matter that was once living, indicated that Otzi was almost 1,000 years older than that, making him the oldest human mummy *ever* found!

For centuries, it was believed that humans' use of metals like copper didn't begin until *after* 2500 B.C.E. Yet Otzi proves that humans of that time were much more advanced than anyone had ever thought.

PUTTING OTZI'S PUZZLE TOGETHER

Scientists learned many other things about the shriveled, dark, little man. Otzi was about forty-five years old when he died on that high mountain pass. He had tattoos on his ankles, knees, and other body parts.

Scientists looked inside Otzi's stomach and found out that the last thing he ate was some sort of grain, some vegetables, and some goat meat. Otzi looked pretty healthy for someone who had been dead for more than 5,000 years! This brought up yet another mystery: However in the world did Otzi die?

CREATURE FEATURE

The history of humankind is divided into ages, or periods of time. The ages change names based on how far humans had developed. That can mean using tools, creating art, languages, etc. In order, the ages are: Paleolithic (Stone) Age, Mesolithic Age, Neolithic Age, Chalcolithic Period, Copper Age, Bronze Age, and Iron Age.

23

LYING AROUND FOR 5,000 YEARS

Doctors carefully looked over Otzi and found no wounds on his body and no injuries to his skull. Special X rays did find a broken rib, and other signs showed that Otzi had held his side for a long time, perhaps because of the pain from the broken rib.

Scientists believe that Otzi had some kind of run-in with a person or an animal and fled to the mountains. There, he probably got caught in a snowstorm and died. His body then lay there for thousands of years.

Incredibly, Otzi was like a man in a time machine. He was so perfectly preserved it was as if he had stepped from the distant past into our world, ready to share what life was like thousands of years ago!

Otzi proved to be a treasure trove of information about life in that long-ago time. He wore a cloak of waterproof reeds, showing that people were inventive in making their clothing. His coat and leggings were made from the fur of an animal, and his leather shoes were stuffed with grass to help ward off the cold. He carried an ax and some arrows and a bow, which he was in the middle of making, showing how people created these important tools.

Flower pollen found in Otzi's clothing showed that he lived in the valley below the mountain pass and also showed that he died in the spring. Flecks of wheat in his coat showed that he lived in a community that farmed wheat, something scientists hadn't thought people could do that long ago!

Today, Otzi is still frozen . . . and still teaching people! He's on display at a museum in Italy in a specially made steel chamber that is kept at 21.2 degrees Fahrenheit at all times. Otzi is still at rest, but his discovery opened up a window into the past, thanks to the amazing preservation of his body by the forces of nature.

MUMMIES OF THE AMERICAS

The high and dry mountains of Central and South America have been the site of numerous discoveries of mummies over the years. The Chachapoya people in the Andes buried their dead in cold, dry caves, where the atmosphere mummified the corpses. However, most mummies were removed and reburied before scientists could study them in detail.

Farther south is the land that formerly belonged to the Incas, another ancient people. When a volcanic eruption spewed hot ash on neighboring mountains in the Peruvian Andes, it melted a thick snowcap, uncovering the earth. Scientists exploring these mountains found a body wrapped in cloth. To their stunned surprise, they found themselves looking into the near-lifelike face of a young girl. They called the mummy Juanita.

Juanita brought up one mysterious question: How did a lone girl come to be high atop the mountain? The answer was as scary as *any* mummy movie.

CREATURE FEATURE

Did you know that the mummy Juanita was displayed in Washington, D.C., to show people what she looked like? Hillary Clinton, who was then the First Lady of the United States, visited and said that Juanita "took my breath away." Eventually, the mummy was returned for safekeeping to Peru.

HUMAN SACRIFICE?

Juanita looked to be about fourteen or fifteen years old when she died in what scientists guess was about 1470. More than 500 years later, Juanita's frozen skin was brown and leathery, but one could still see that she had black hair. Her teeth were visible, along with her high cheekbones. She was wrapped in a brown-and-white cloth. To carry her down the mountain, scientists wrapped the hundred-pound mummy in a pink insulated blanket and put the body in a special backpack.

In a lab in North Carolina, scientists used X rays and CAT scans to peer inside Juanita's skeleton. To their horror, they discovered that she had been murdered with a terrible blow to her head!

Scientists believe that Incas practiced human sacrifice and that Juanita may have been a victim of the practice. Perhaps she was killed in a way that the Incas thought would please their gods. Poor Juanita!

THE BOG PEOPLE

Juanita and Otzi were turned into mummies by the dry, freezing-cold conditions high atop mountains. But there's another, *totally different* natural process that preserves bodies in other parts of the world! Meet some of the best-preserved mummies around: the Bog People!

In many countries in Europe, large areas of land — "bogs" — are covered by a substance called peat. Peat is thick, brown, mudlike stuff that is made up mainly of decomposed plants. The plants in this wet land change into a heavy substance that some local people cut and dry and then burn for fuel.

But things other than plants sometimes fall into the soupy mess. And they don't come out until people dig them out! One of these "things" went into the bog as a man, but he came out as a *mummy*!

TOLLUND MAN

In 1950, some men were digging peat in a bog called Tollund Fen, near Silkeborg, Denmark. About nine feet down, one of their triangular iron blades struck a soft bundle of cloth. What was inside stunned the men — and *still* amazes scientists! The man inside the bundle was one of the most beautifully preserved mummies ever found.

"Tollund Man" looks like a bronze statue, with every whisker on his face visible. His skin is dark brown, a reaction to the tannic acid produced by the bog. He has

BIZARRO-RAMA: QUICK QUIZ

Peat moss — the same stuff that helped preserve Tollund Man and other mummies — helps keep wounds infection-free. True or false?

(Answer: True. Doctors working on soldiers in World War I sometimes used peat moss to wrap wounds to help them heal more quickly!)

a lined forehead, a large nose, and lips that look chapped in an *eerily* lifelike way. He looks remarkably like people who still live in the region. In fact, some believe he could walk around Silkeborg today (if he could) and no one would look twice!

He might want to get dressed first, though! The powerful acid in the bog destroyed his clothes, but not the items made of leather, so Tollund Man was found with a two-inch-wide leather belt around his middle and a peaked leather hat. He looks as if he has just lain down for a nap, but in fact, he's been dead for more than 2,400 years! Although Tollund Man looks peaceful, his death was *anything* but. . . .

GRISLY MYSTERIES

If you look closely at Tollund Man's neck you can see the rope that was used to hang him! But why? There is no evidence to show why he was put to death. Was he a criminal? Or was his death part of some sort of sacrifice, like Juanita's? No one will ever know for sure.

Oddly, several other bog mummies also show signs of execution. The 2,000-year-old Elling Woman, found in Scandinavia, was also hanged. The

Grauballe Man, found in France, had his throat cut around 300 B.C.E.

To this day, the mummies found in bogs hold more mysteries than other natural mummies — because investigators still don't know how those mummies got there.

DESERT MUMMIES

The hot, dry air of deserts also keeps bodies from decomposing. Who knows how many mummies are hidden in the vast sands of the world's huge deserts?

One group of mummies was found in a desert, but they weren't nearly as *old* as most mummies. These mummies, discovered in the African nation of Libya, were soldiers from World War II. In 1943, a B-24 Liberator bomber called the *Lady Be Good* disappeared while returning to the base. No one knew what had

CREATURE FEATURE

Scientists discovering the ill-fated crewmen in Libya were helped by an important artifact. A diary found near the mummies told the story of the men's courageous, but unsuccessful trek!

happened to the plane or where the men on board had gone — until 1958, that is, when explorers found the wreckage of the plane in the desert. But there were no remains of humans to be found.

Where had the airmen gone? Into the desert, to become the most modern mummies ever found.

A FATEFUL TRIP

In 1960, another crew of explorers found some of the human remains. The airmen had apparently tried to walk out of the burning hot desert. Alone, without water, without food, they had no chance. One by one, they died and collapsed into the scorching desert sands. When their bodies were found, they had become mummies. Their bare ribs showed above the sand, but below it, they were as preserved as any mummies found in bogs or caves. The dry air and fierce wind had combined with the hot sand to mummify the men.

Unlike the other mummies in this book, who lived hundreds or thousands of years ago, these mummies were not to end up in a museum. Instead, they were returned home to be buried properly and honored as heroes, with their coffins covered with American flags.

WRAP-UP

Wind, cold, heat, and other conditions can turn dead human bodies into natural mummies. When old mummies are found, they are fascinating beings, weird to look at but interesting to study.

But more importantly, they are people. And people tell stories — stories of long ago about life before e-mail, telephones, cars, and even electricity. These amazing mummies can show us where we as humans came from . . . and where, perhaps, we may be going!

3

ALIENS IN AMERICA

For more than fifty years, the question of what – or who – landed in Roswell, New Mexico, has been hotly debated. Was it actually a spaceship containing aliens, as some swear? Or was it all an innocent test conducted by the government? You decide!

STRANGE VISITORS

When you hear the word *alien* today, you might think of great films like *E.T.*, *Close Encounters of the Third Kind*, or the *Men in Black* movies. But for residents of Roswell, New Mexico, back in 1947, "close encounters" went *way* beyond something you see in the movies! Many still insist that the desert town of Roswell was the scene of an authentic alien visitation. Today, what is now known as "the Roswell Incident" remains one of the most fascinating — *and controversial* — of history's mysteries.

LOOK! UP IN THE SKY!

Is it a bird? A plane? Or a flying saucer? Throughout the years, witnesses who have seen unidentified flying objects (UFOs) report that they look like saucers, rockets, solid clouds, and even giant cigars! Others say they've spied strange aircraft that looked like giant disks — think of a huge Frisbee sailing through the sky. Pilots have reported seeing these unexplained vessels flying high in the air. Other people have spotted them skimming closer to the ground. Normally, UFOs are spotted flying through the air.

But in the famous 1940s case of Roswell, a UFO is said to have done much more than fly. It actually *landed* in a stretch of ranch land in the New Mexico desert! Or, more accurately, it *crashed*. . . .

CREATURE FEATURE

Reports of visitors from other planets have been around as long as man. Ancient Hindu texts from around 3000 B.C.E. tell of strange things appearing in the sky, and some scientists believe that mysterious miles-long lines in the ground in South America were made by extraterrestrials!

UNEXPLAINED SIGHTINGS

What became the most famous of all UFO sightings first began around June 25, 1947. Numerous people in and around Roswell, New Mexico, reported seeing strange objects flying in the sky. Many said they saw silver saucers zipping across the heavens at high speed. Newspapers even reported that people feared Martians were invading Earth!

Then, on July 5, something really *did* fall from the skies near Roswell, landing on a field owned by a sheep rancher, Mac Brazel. Believing that the material he found in his field was debris from a flying saucer, Mac asked the local sheriff to come out and investigate.

The sheriff called in officers from the nearby Roswell Air Force Base, who took the debris away to their base. And that's when the mystery, which has con-

BIZARRO-RAMA: QUICK QUIZ

UFOlogy is the study of UFOs, and UFOlogists are people who study these mysterious visitors from outer space. True or false?

(Answer: True)

tinued for decades, began. What, exactly, *did* the sheriff and his men take back to that base?

OFFICIALLY ALIENS?!

On July 8, 1947, the U.S. Air Force issued a press release, an official document alerting reporters to a piece of news. And what a piece of news it was! "We have retrieved a flying saucer," the report said. It set off a stampede of reporters and other curious people to the sleepy town of Roswell.

"When [the] story went out . . . it was a bombshell," says alien investigator Donald J. Burleson, Ph.D. "All of a sudden the whole world was hearing this business about a flying saucer."

CREATURE FEATURE

To this day, every July Fourth weekend, thousands of people flock to Roswell to commemorate the anniversary of what they believe is the most important UFO event ever recorded!

But just as suddenly as the excitement began, it was over. The U.S. Air Force issued another press release, which said the silvery debris was not a UFO, but pieces of a broken weather balloon. But was it really?

ALIENS ABDUCTED?

The "incident" might have ended then and there. But a book in 1980 revealed some very interesting information about visitors from another world! Charles Berlitz's book *The Roswell Incident* says that U.S. Air Force officers took a lot more than just parts of a flying saucer out of the field. Charles Berlitz claims they actually took the *bodies of aliens* killed in the crash!

Witnesses now say that there were many military personnel on the site soon after the crash who took away parts of the crashed craft as well as alien bodies. Some witnesses even claim that

BIZARRO-RAMA: QUICK QUIZ

The U.S. Air Force and some scientific groups still use huge, helium-filled balloons to help learn about the weather and about wind patterns. The balloons rise up high in the air and transmit data back to computers on the ground. True or false?

(Answer: True)

one of the aliens was alive, and that it tried to talk to the officers!

But these saucer parts and alien bodies were never displayed to the public. Some people believe the U.S. Air Force may have been hiding something: that the aliens were *real*.

CREATURES FROM ANOTHER PLANET?

The people who saw what was left after the Roswell crash gave detailed descriptions of seeing mangled bodies with oversized heads. Witnesses agreed that the aliens had no hair, no eyelashes or eyebrows, and no visible ears. Their hands had four fingers. Their faces had blank expressions, resembling dummies or dolls, and they wore one-piece suits with no markings.

"The creatures were of very short stature. No more probably than three and a half feet," says Dr. Burleson. The head of an alien was described as pear-shaped, with larger-than-usual eyes, a barely visible mouth, and not much for ears or nose.

MONSTER-SIZE CREATURE FEATURE

Was the silvery debris in Roswell really a weather balloon? A 1995 report by the U.S. Air Force said that the debris wasn't actually a weather balloon, but a secret spy experiment called Project Mogul. This experiment tested balloons and other flying devices as a way to watch for missiles from other countries. The scientists tied silver balloons to long strings and floated instruments up into the sky. The balloons looked like floating silver jellyfish, and the government says this is what - people saw when they claimed to see UFOs! The government says the balloon that crashed into Mac Brazel's field was one of the Project Mogul devices. It contained odd machines, weird materials, and strange pink-and-purple designs — which viewers might have thought were created by aliens!

They certainly were like no other pilots on Earth! So what *were* these bizarre beings?

CRASH-TEST DUMMIES?

The government had a logical answer for this mystery. The "aliens" seen in Roswell were actually special crash-test dummies!

A U.S. Air Force report issued in 1997 said the military had been testing a type of parachute designed to operate at very high altitudes. It was too dangerous to test on humans, so they created lifelike dummies. They strapped the dummies into the chutes and dropped them from enormous heights. Guess where they said many of them landed. That's right . . . near Roswell!

And they say the dummies had no hair, no ears, small mouths, and wore one-piece suits. Sound familiar?

Witnesses said that the bodies were "cold to the touch," and the U.S. Air Force said this was because the dummies had plummeted from high in the atmosphere, where the temperature is well below freezing. As far as the U.S. Air Force was concerned, the case was closed. Or was it?

DUMMY TROUBLE

Dr. Burleson points out that witnesses said the aliens were very short, but that the dummies were six feet tall or more! Also, the parachute experiments didn't begin until 1954, *seven years* after the aliens landed in Roswell.

So were there really aliens in Roswell — or not? Few are convinced by the "crash-test dummy" explanation. They just think it's too easy for the government to come up with new stories to disprove what the witnesses think is real: that aliens really did land on Earth.

CREATURE FEATURE

Thousands of objects from outer space hit Earth every year. But they're not filled with aliens . . . they're just big rocks. Meteorites smash into Earth's atmosphere and burn up. Some tiny rocks do get through and land, usually in the ocean. Some scientists blame an enormous meteor for causing a worldwide dust cloud that wiped out the dinosaurs sixty-five million years ago!

And according to one witness who claims to have seen the alien bodies *up close* himself, they were nearly the last thing he saw in his life!

41

A TIMELY WITNESS

Glenn Dennis worked at a mortuary near Roswell. A mortuary is a place where dead bodies are prepared for funeral services. Dennis says that the day after the crash, he drove an airman to the Roswell Air Force Base, and when he arrived, he saw things he couldn't *believe*.

In the back of an ambulance on the base, Glenn saw strange debris with weird writing. When Glenn went into the hospital to check it out, an Army captain angrily chased him out, threatening, "They're gonna be picking *your* bones out of the sand," if he talked about what he'd seen. When Dennis returned the next day, a nurse told him a story that boggles the mind. . . .

BIZARRO-RAMA: QUICK QUIZ

The first mammal to travel to outer space in a rocket ship was a rabbit. True or false?

(Answer: False. It was a monkey!)

AN ALIEN AUTOPSY

After a body dies, doctors sometimes perform what is called an autopsy, which means they use surgical instruments to look inside it and find out

MONSTER-SIZE CREATURE FEATURE

Did Glenn Dennis see real aliens? In 1956, a horrible crash killed eleven U.S. Air Force crewmen near Roswell. There was a terrible fire, and the bodies were badly burned. Military personnel worked hard to keep people away from the scene.

Later, at the hospital, surgeons working on the bodies had to stop their autopsy because of the overpowering smell of jet fuel. The bodies were sent to the same funeral home where Dennis worked.

Also, in 1959, a U.S. Air Force parachutist crash-landed and was badly injured. His head swelled up grotesquely and he was wrapped in bandages to ease the swelling. The government says Dennis simply mixed up these two incidents in his mind and "created" his version of the alien autopsy events. We may never know for certain which explanation is the *real* one.

why it died. The nurse told Dennis she'd witnessed an autopsy on *alien* bodies!

The nurse said that there were two mutilated, very small bodies on the gurney. The bodies looked like they were almost black. The smell was so overpowering in the operating room that the surgeons had to stop the autopsy in the middle! The bodies were then taken to the funeral home. Dennis was shocked by the nurse's story.

Strangely, the next day, the nurse was shipped out, and was never heard from again. Was she hidden away for telling Dennis her story?

MORE SIGHTINGS!

The controversy over the smashed "flying saucer" and the tiny, mangled bodies continues today. People still report UFOs, and Roswell remains a popular spot to see them. Thousands of visitors flock to the town each year, stores sell tons of souvenirs with drawings of the aliens, and a popular museum even displays alien-search artifacts!

Still, many say there's nothing *really* alien up in the sky and never was. "We flew a number of disk-shaped objects," says one scientist. "And those were seen in the air, sometimes as flying saucers."

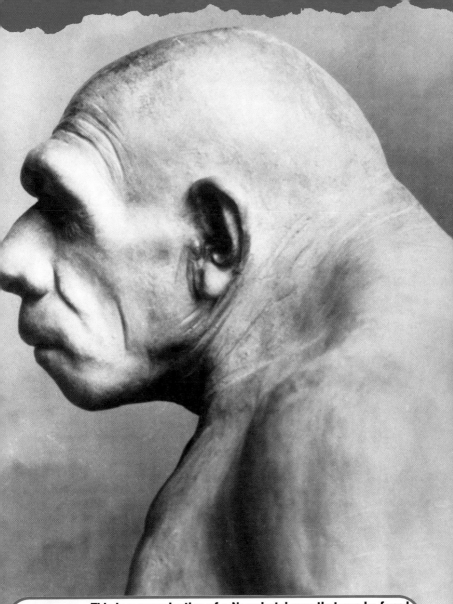

THE HISTORY CHANNEL

This is a reproduction of a Neandertal man that can be found in the Chicago Field Museum. Through careful research and the lucky discovery of fossilized bones, scientists have been able to re-create what our cavemen ancestors looked like . . . and it's not a pretty sight!

This picture, taken from the 1944 movie *The Mummy's Ghost*, shows actor Lon Chaney wrapped up in special gauze to play the scary mummy, Kharis. When most people hear the word *mummy*, they think of this kind of monster. But Mother Nature, it seems, offers a very different sort of mummy, such as the Tollund Man (see next photo).

THE HISTORY CHANNEL.

Photofest

 THE HISTORY CHANNEL® The "Tollund Man," found in Denmark in 1950, looks like he's just taking a peaceful nap—even though he's been dead for more than 2,400 years. Talk about creepy!

So far, we have no conclusive proof that aliens do exist. This picture shows a re-creation of an alien figure that was done using an alien doll. Many people think aliens probably look like this — and the witnesses of the Roswell Incident swear that the alien bodies were bald, short figures who had enormous eyes!

THE ROSWELL REPORT

CASE CLOSED

On Tuesday, June 24, 1997, the U.S. Air Force released "The Roswell Report," in which the Air Force attempted to close the mysterious case that had been open since 1947. In the 231-page report, the Air Force explains that extraterrestrial bodies were not found near Roswell, New Mexico. What do *you* believe?

This giant octopus (*Octopus dofleini*) can be found swimming in the waters near Alaska. The seas and oceans of the world are swarming with creepy creatures . . . and this is just one spine-chilling example! In for a swim?

 THE HISTORY CHANNEL

This is the famous "Surgeon's" photograph of the Loch Ness monster, taken on April 19, 1934, by Robert Kenneth Wilson. Seeing the photo for yourself, what do you think is the truth about Nessie?

Some say that the Loch Ness monster is a plesiosaur—a type of dinosaur—which has mysteriously survived all these years. This illustration shows plesiosaurs swimming. These water-loving dinosaurs do look a lot like Nessie, don't they?

DO YOU BELIEVE?

Did aliens *actually* land in Roswell? Are there UFOs flying around us? Which story do you think is true?

"I wish we had a piece of debris," says Dr. Burleson. "I wish we had a photograph of the crash site before the retrieval [of the saucer] . . . I wish we had a photograph of the body . . . I wish we had the bodies, but we don't have any of those things.

"I would say the Roswell crash is the most significant event in human history," Dr. Burleson adds. "We had an encounter with creatures from another world."

So, now that you've read all the evidence . . . what do *you* believe?

45

4

"BEYOND HERE BE MONSTERS": CREATURES OF THE DEEP

Oceans and deep-water lakes are said to be *teeming* with all sorts of creepy creatures – from descendants of strange prehistoric fish to giant squid. And these watery wonders are often downright *monstrous!*

WATER MONSTERS: A SHORT HISTORY

Ever since people have sailed the seas, they have come home with fantastic stories of wild and mysterious creatures living in the water. Some old maps even have a line running through an ocean that shows how ships traveled. On the other side of the line, the mapmakers wrote: *Beyond Here Be Monsters!*

46

Daryl Ligasan

Even peaceful lakes were thought to be the homes of monsters. The deep, dark waters sheltered animals that were only rarely seen, but which many people feared. These freshwater creatures were believed to be every bit as dangerous as their saltwater counterparts. And every bit as mysterious . . .

Today, scientific investigations have solved some of the old mysteries, and many of the "monsters" have been identified as interesting species of fish or mammal. But the world's seas and lakes *still* contain unexplained bizarre beings.

THE "CHAMP" OF THE LAKE

The craggy shore of Lake Champlain lies between Vermont and New York in the northeast corner of the United States. The 109-mile-long lake is more than 400 feet deep. With hundreds of secluded coves and deep inlets, the lake is full of fish and plants, which means there are plenty of places for a creature to hide and enough food for it to eat. And many people think a creature is indeed hiding out in Lake Champlain!

"Champ" (also known as "Champy") is a very bizarre being that supposedly has been seen by hundreds of people

CREATURE FEATURE

Cryptozoologists are the scientists who study unknown or very unusual animals. Using modern techniques like sonar, radar, and video along with historical research, they travel to the ends of the earth to track creatures. All of the creatures in this chapter are the subjects of cryptozoological investigation. If you like this book, maybe you'd want to consider a career as a cryptozoologist!

over the years. Thought by some to be a very large, dinosaurlike reptile, Champy is a sleek, dark animal with a long neck!

CHAMP'S TALE

Lake Champlain is named for French explorer Samuel de Champlain, who was the first person ever to write about Champ. In 1609 Champlain made an entry in his journal describing a long, reptilelike creature crossing the lake. But scientists today think what he saw was a gigantic fish with jagged teeth called a garpike.

BIZARRO-RAMA: QUICK QUIZ

The Vermont Expos minor-league baseball team has a cartoon picture of Champ on their hats and even has a person wearing a Champ costume dance on the dugout during games. True or false?

(Answer: True. So even if Champ isn't real, at least he has a job!)

In 1821, a boatman rowing across the lake reported nearly running into a giant, slumbering creature that looked like a dinosaur! Many years later, Sheriff Nathan H. Mooney observed the same odd-looking creature from about fifty feet away. He said the creature was about thirty feet long, with a long neck and small head. Could it have been Champy?

CHAMP'S CHAMPION

"Champ" is a popular part of local Vermont lore, and many residents claim to have seen the creature. Dennis Hall says he has seen the elusive Champ more than twenty-five times. He describes one close-up encounter on a misty night in the reeds along the banks of Lake Champlain.

CREATURE FEATURE

A woman named Sandra Mansi took a photograph of Champ in 1977, which showed the creature in Lake Champlain. The photo was analyzed by scientists at the Smithsonian Institution and by photo experts. Their conclusion? The photograph was *not* faked.

"I was walking along the edge of the marsh. . . . When I first came up to it, I couldn't see anything. I could smell it, though. It smelled like a snake, a very strong smell, almost as strong as a skunk. And there [was] splashing in the marsh. So I went and got a flashlight and I could see those red eyes looking at me. I could see it, I could hear it, I could smell it. It was frightening." But was it real? No one really knows for sure . . .

A SLIPPERY SEA SERPENT

Not far from Champ's home in Vermont is the rugged coast of Massachusetts. For more than 300 years, residents there have reported seeing what they have come to call the Great New England Sea Serpent. This bizarre being makes its home in the salty ocean.

BIZARRO-RAMA: QUICK QUIZ

Most cryptozoologists don't believe that Champ and other lake creatures are prehistoric animals. True or false?

(Answer: False. Scientists believe that these bizarre beings are descendants of prehistoric creatures!)

Reports from early colonial times in New England mention a thin, snakelike animal that stretched almost a *mile* long! In 1817, a serpent remained in Gloucester Harbor for more than a month. Hundreds of people saw a creature with a large head, bright eyes, and a long, scaly body slinking back and forth in the harbor. Years later, British ships reported that a huge serpent passed their boat not far off the coast.

There are hundreds of species of weird creatures in the world's waters. Is the Great New England Sea Serpent an undiscovered species? Or something left over from the prehistoric past?

VISIBLE IN VANCOUVER

The cold waters of Cadboro Bay off Vancouver Island in Victoria, British Columbia, are home to another famous water monster. Nicknamed "Caddy," the creature is said to be long and thick, with a wide, flat head with ridges on its back. Its head is said to look like a horse or large goat, and some witnesses

CREATURE FEATURE

The famous circus owner P. T. Barnum was famous for putting unusual things on display and calling them real monsters! Another trick he played on customers was directing them to one such creature with a huge sign: THIS WAY TO THE EGRESS! People would go out the door and find themselves outside. An egress is not an animal . . . it's another word for exit!

have seen short flippers on the front part of its body.

Though reports of Caddy have been found as far back as the 1830s, the sightings really picked up in the 1930s. That was when a specimen of the creature was actually found by whalers.

NAME THAT MONSTER!

In 1937, a group of whalers killed a giant sperm whale off the coast of British Columbia. When they cut open its stomach, out slid an unknown creature nearly fourteen feet long, an odd lunch for a whale! In their long years at sea, the experienced fishermen had seen nearly every creature in the area . . . but *never* one like this!

But before scientists could check it out or take accurate photographs, it vanished. Did Caddy just not want to be seen? Where did she go? Though Caddy was never "captured" again, people continue to report sightings of the serpent.

BIZARRO-RAMA: QUICK QUIZ
Caddy's official name is *Cadborasaurus willsi*. True or false?

(Answer: True)

YOU GO, OGOPOGO!

For thousands of years, Native Americans crossing Lake Okanagan in British Columbia made sure to bring a meal for the mighty monster that lived in the dark, cold waters. By tossing in some meat as they rowed their canoes, the natives hoped that the monster — later known as Ogopogo — wouldn't make *them* its latest meal!

MONSTER LEGEND?

The Native American elders told young people the story of Na-ha-tiq, which means "snake in the water." They said that the creature was part god and part demon, both good and bad. But many think these fables of the Okanagan were made up to keep children from going out into the dangerous water.

Ogopogo *was* just another legend until 1856, when a man named John McDougall was crossing the lake with two horses swimming behind, tied to his canoe. McDougall hadn't brought a snack for Na-ha-tiq . . . so Na-ha-tiq had his horses for lunch!

The two animals suddenly disappeared beneath the surface of the water, and McDougall's canoe tipped up into the air! If he hadn't been able to

MONSTER-SIZE CREATURE FEATURE

In 1819, the Nantucket whale ship *Essex* set out to track down the earth's largest creature . . . and met with *doom* just fifteen months later! While in the South Pacific, sailors harpooned a sperm whale — and it attacked the ship! The enraged whale slammed into the ship again and again until it *sank*. The crew ended up in the three tiny lifeboats for three months, sailing 4,500 miles toward South America. Many of the men died. But some survived . . . because they resorted to cannibalism — eating their dead shipmates — when there was no food left!

slice the rope in an instant, he might have joined his horses at the bottom of the lake. What — or *who* — was under there? Could it have been Ogopogo?

PEEKING AT 'POGO

Descriptions of Ogopogo vary widely. Some say the creature is dark green, others say brownish.

Some witnesses say it's twenty feet long and others say seventy. But regardless of what it looks like, many say they have *definitely* encountered the creature!

One woman saw it surfacing like a fish — but it kept going, until thirty feet of Ogopogo was above the water! Another woman claims that when she was swimming, she was thrown out of the water when the animal came up underneath her.

From an ancient legend told around campfires to video footage shown on TV, Ogopogo has continued to live. But whether it lives in real life or just imagination . . . well, that debate continues!

FRIEND OF THE DINOSAURS

"Monsters" like Caddy, Champ, and Ogopogo remain mysterious because science has yet to prove that they're real. Many people have seen these creatures, but no one has ever taken one into captivity.

But scientists have nabbed other amazing creatures of the deep. These wild animals might be the source of other sea monster stories. One such *incredible* fish is the coelacanth.

Scientists thought this fish with thick scales and sharp teeth had disappeared sixty million years ago. It was all over the world in prehistoric times, about 360 million years ago. But no one in our time had seen one *alive*.

But in 1938, off the coast of South Africa, a fishing boat hauled something very strange on board. It was a coelacanth, thought to be extinct! Since then, more than 200 coelacanths have been preserved in museums worldwide.

BIZARRO-RAMA: QUICK QUIZ

If you sank Mount Everest into the deepest part of the ocean, it would stick up out of the water.
True or false?

(Answer: False. The ocean is about a mile deeper than the height of Mount Everest!)

MEET MEGAMOUTH

If the coelacanth had survived all those years undetected, another, larger reptile could be around as well. The discovery of the coelacanth excited cryptozoologists, and they searched even harder for new species.

Another extraordinary discovery of a prehistoric sea creature occurred in 1978, when a U.S. Navy ship found a shark in the waters near Hawaii. But it wasn't a shark anyone had *ever*

seen before! The animal was a fearsome, sixteen-foot creature with an *enormous* gaping jaw, which was dubbed "Megamouth."

There are other fish that scientists thought were relatives of creatures like Champ and Caddy. For example, oarfish can be up to twenty-five feet long but only *one foot wide*! Oarfish look like gray ribbons waving through the water, their huge gray eyes helping them live deep beneath the ocean. Could the oarfish be one of the "sea serpents" people feared long ago?

CREATURE FEATURE

As far back as ancient Greece and Rome, seamen were worried that a giant squid would grab their boats. With tentacles reaching more than fifty feet long, the creepy-looking sea creatures were the stuff of terrifying legend. Actually, real squid couldn't grab more than a rowboat . . . but sailors feared the squid anyway!

WHO'S NEXT?

Along with the hundreds of thousands of amazing aquatic creatures in the world, from coelacanths to squids, scientists discover more than *one hundred* new species of underwater creatures every year. Some are former "monsters" of long ago, and some are just little fish.

The sightings will continue, too, and the search for further evidence of "real" sea monsters will go on until someone actually catches one. Who knows? The next new species they discover might live in a lake in Canada or the United States . . . or in an ocean near you!

BIZARRO-RAMA: QUICK QUIZ

According to the *Guinness Book of World Records*, the animal with the largest eye in the animal kingdom is the giant squid. True or false?

(Answer: *True:* At seventeen inches across, it's bigger than a dinner plate!)

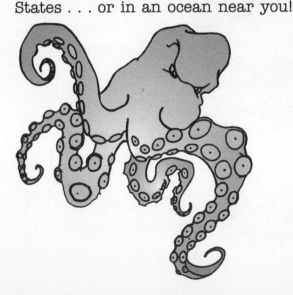

5

NESSIE: THE WORLD'S MOST BIZARRE BEING?

Now that you've read about all the creepy monsters that slink through the world's waters, get ready to meet the creepiest – and most mysterious – sea creature of them all. In a lake in Scotland, many say there lives a strange, long-necked beast who goes by the name of Nessie. What Nessie is, and if she is real, is a mystery that continues today. Read on to meet the famous Loch Ness Monster!

A VERY OLD MYSTERY

For more than 1,500 years, reports of a huge creature that lives in the deep, cold depths of Scotland's Loch Ness have been at the center of a serious controversy. Over the years, scientists, writers, and researchers have come to the lake in search of the ancient creature. And while some see "Nessie" as a fanciful old myth, others have been willing to risk everything to prove that the creature lives on.

HOME TO A MONSTER?

One of the largest, deepest lakes in Europe is Scotland's Loch Ness. The lake is at the center of a sixty-mile-long crevice in the earth called the Great Glen. This enormous ditch was formed millions of years ago when massive glaciers melted away, leaving giant holes filled with seawater.

CREATURE FEATURE

In Wales, an annual race is held in a peat bog. Competitors swim through smelly, brown, insect-filled, peat-thick water for a prize of only a few dollars and a pint of ice cream! Do you think it's worth the grossout experience?

Over time, Loch Ness changed from salt water to freshwater, forming a lake twenty-two miles long, a mile wide, and anywhere from 500 to 800 feet deep. Peat — soil made of decomposed plants and animals that has built up over thousands of soggy years — lines the lake, turning the water a bizarre brown. (As you may recall from the *Mummies* chapter in this book, peat has preserved dead people in some places around the world!)

Scottish historians from the 1700s and 1800s wrote about strange sights around the Loch Ness. These included sightings of "waves without wind" and "fish without fin." Could these have been signs of a monster?

THE ROAD TO NESSIE

It was in 1933 that the road that runs around Loch Ness was widened and improved. More travelers started coming to the scenic area, and the views of the lake became much better.

BIZARRO-RAMA: QUICK QUIZ

Nessie could be a whale that slipped into the loch at one time. True or false?

(Answer: False. Nessie certainly is the size of a whale, but the canals are much smaller, and no whale could have navigated them!)

"Prior to that, if you drove what little road there was, it was mainly obscured by bushes, trees, and so on," says Loch Ness Monster investigator Roy Mackal. "Now, if you drive around the loch, you can see into it from most of the distance around the loch."

62

On April 14, 1933, Mr. and Mrs. John Mackay were driving home on Highway 98 on the Northeast side of the loch. Gazing out the window, Mrs. Mackay noticed a strange commotion in the water. And what was it that Mrs. Mackay believed she saw? "The beast," she declared. Her sighting led a reporter from the nearby *Inverness Chronicle* to write a story in his paper. And in that article, for the first time, the mysterious, dark creature swimming in the Scottish lake got a name. The hunt was on to find the "Loch Ness Monster!"

WIT-"NESSIES"

Many more local people reported seeing odd things in the loch. Some saw humps or bumps rolling through the water! Other witnesses claimed that they had also seen flippers or a tail. A few sharp-eyed eyewitnesses said they saw the creature's head and neck.

CREATURE FEATURE

Want to look for Nessie yourself without leaving your school or home? Visit www.lochness. scotland.net and see the live WebCam shots of Loch Ness. Who knows? Maybe Nessie will pick that moment to show herself. A girl from Texas says she saw the head and neck in a WebCam photograph in 1999!

"We saw this great neck emerge from the water at least five feet, we estimate, above the water," says one witness. "It was moving slowly toward the middle of the loch, rather slowly for about twenty seconds."

More stories appeared, and as publicity spread, the monster got her famous nickname of Nessie. Newspapers all over Great Britain picked up the story, and tales of the mysterious thing swimming in Loch Ness began to create headlines in newspapers worldwide. But what were all these witnesses *really* seeing?

A "NESSIE-SAURUS"?

At first, descrip-

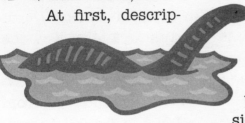

tions of the lake creature sounded like an ancient reptile called the plesiosaur that lived in the time of the dinosaurs. The plesiosaur lived in oceans and large lakes, grew to more than sixty feet in length, and had a long neck, flippers, and a thin tail. It used its huge flippers to "sail" quickly through the water with what scientists believe was a swimming motion.

Many of these details matched up to the accounts of Nessie witnesses. But how could a dinosaur have survived for so long in one lake? Scientists were stumped by this puzzle.

Another theory was that a big seal had slipped into the lake, but seals are ocean creatures and probably would not survive in the freshwater of Loch Ness. Freshwater otters in Scotland's rivers sometimes grew to be eight feet long or more, but they did not have the long necks or flippers that people were seeing. The mystery remained and the debate raged on.

FOOD AND FAMILY

If there was a huge monster living in Loch Ness, what did it *eat*? Where did it sleep? Did it have a family? These questions rang across the world after the Mackay sighting.

Salmon and other fish are plentiful in Loch Ness, so it seems certain that if Nessie is real, she has plenty of fishy choices for breakfast, lunch, *and* dinner! As for her "home," Loch Ness is very deep, with steeply sloping sides that may contain caves or hollows where Nessie can hide out.

Some observers felt that there must be a small family of the beasts, reproducing once in a while to bring new Nessies into the world. No Nessie babies have ever been found, but if there are strange creatures

BIZARRO-RAMA: QUICK QUIZ

If Nessie really *is* a leftover dinosaur, then the last time she lived with other dinosaurs would have been about one thousand years ago. True or false?

(Answer: False. Try one million years ago!)

in Loch Ness today, they're probably not the same Nessies that people in the 1930s saw!

As the debate continued about what or who Nessie was, things suddenly got more mysterious when the first pictures of "her" surfaced.

ON CAMERA

In December 1933, several out-of-focus pictures and a few seconds of grainy, jumpy film that allegedly showed Nessie came to light. The creature appeared to be giant, long-necked, dark-skinned, and shiny. Not long after the first photographs appeared, a London newspaper called *The Daily Mail* decided to do something more than just print pictures and stories. They decided to *find* the creature!

MARMADUKE'S MISSION

Marmaduke Wetherall was not just a hunter who chased big game around the world. He was also a movie director with a flair for the dramatic. *The Daily Mail* hired Wetherall and covered his trip to the loch in great detail with reporters and photographers.

Only days after beginning his search in late 1933, Wetherall struck monster gold. He found a footprint at the edge of the loch that appeared to be from some giant, unknown creature. Within

67

a week, as news of the discovery spread, the entire area was flooded with monster-hunters.

Unfortunately, only a couple of weeks later, Wetherall was blown out of the water, so to speak. A careful study of the footprint by the British Museum came up with a stunning conclusion: It

MONSTER-SIZE CREATURE FEATURE

In the spring of 1934, a Scottish doctor named Robert Kenneth Wilson brought forward a black-and-white photograph that would become *hugely* famous. The bottom center of the frame showed what looked like the head and neck of a dark-colored creature rising out of the water. The small head of the creature points to the right at the end of a long, dinosaurlike neck. It also looks as if the creature is swimming across the lake, with most of its body below the surface. Was this the first real photograph of the Loch Ness Monster? Millions of people thought so, and the "Surgeon's Photo" became the most famous picture ever taken of Nessie!

was not made by a monster at all. Someone had made the footprint by using a stuffed hippopotamus.

Although Wetherall was fired by *The Daily Mail*, the damage was done. Those people who believed that Nessie was a hoax had more evidence. And even true believers began to wonder.

THE HUNTS CONTINUE

In 1960, Oxford University scientists used underwater echo-sounding gear to show that the lake was big and deep enough to support a creature of Nessie's alleged size. This high-tech equipment sent out sound waves and read the "echoes" of the waves as they bounced off things, from fish to rocks to . . . Nessie?

And on April 23, 1960, British aerospace engineer Tim Dinsdale filmed *something* that he

CREATURE FEATURE

In 1969, a submarine went 600 feet deep into Loch Ness. It spotted *something* swimming about a hundred feet away, went after it . . . and lost it in the deep, dark water! Once again, Nessie remained "at large."

said was the lake monster! His short clip of a large hump moving across the loch was the clearest movie ever of Nessie.

Overnight, Nessie and Dinsdale were famous throughout the world. Experts at the British Royal Air Force studied the film carefully and concluded that the movie *did* record an "animate" object, which means it was alive! And whatever that "animate" creature was, experts said it was twelve feet long and three feet high!

READY FOR HER CLOSE-UP?

In 1972, a scientist using a special underwater camera caught a photograph of what many thought was a still-mysterious beast. The computer-enhanced film showed a flipper-shaped object moving past the camera.

BIZARRO-RAMA: QUICK QUIZ

If Nessie really is a giant amphibious reptile, a salamander might be her "cousin." True or false?

(Answer: *True*)

In 1975, using even more advanced gear, scientists took a photograph that they said was a close-up portrait of Nessie's face. The dark and shadowed figure looked to some like a gargoyle, which is a carving of an ugly beast that appears on old buildings. But some analysts said they could actually see eyes and a nose in the photographs!

OPERATION DEEPSCAN

In 1987, Operation Deepscan was launched. Nineteen powerboats were equipped with echo-sounding devices and deployed in Loch Ness. The boats lined up across the width of the lake, and as they moved down its twenty-two-mile length, every square inch of the undersea area was mapped by the sophisticated devices.

Computers gathered the data from the devices and everyone looked for some clue that Nessie was indeed "down there." The scans detected three large objects in the water, but again, Nessie evaded her hunters.

Was she swimming deep beneath the dark waters of the loch, hiding from the noise of the boats? Did she have a secret tunnel in the bottom of the lake where she could hide? Nessie was still acting shy!

THE TRUTH ABOUT NESSIE?

Today, the search for Nessie continues. She even has an official scientific name: *Nessiteras rhomboptery*. But that doesn't necessarily make

CREATURE FEATURE

The photographs featuring Nessie's face and other evidence of the creature's existence were presented to Britain's House of Commons amid much publicity in the 1970s. But again, nothing about Nessie was proven for certain. In the 1980s, when computers gathered some data about the creature in Loch Ness, all the fancy equipment could not turn up one *solid* piece of evidence that the Loch Ness Monster was real.

her real. Still, dozens of people claim to see some part of Nessie every year, whether from the road around the lake, from the shore, or from the many tour boats that still go out in search of the elusive creature. There is even news of Nessie on the Internet!

Is Nessie a remnant of an ancient dinosaur family that has survived for thousands of years in Loch Ness's dark, cold water? Or is she just a myth built up by people who want to believe in monsters?

Will the Loch Ness Monster someday surface for good to greet the world and prove that she's real? Only Nessie knows for sure. . . .

BIZARRE BEINGS: THE ULTIMATE CHALLENGE

Hey, creature-watchers! Now that you've traveled back in time, gone deep into lakes and oceans, and wandered bogs, tundra, and deserts in search of the most bizarre beings *ever*, why not test what you know? No peeking at the chapters!

1. **Why is 1947 an important year to alien seekers?**
   a. E.T. was born that year.
   b. An alien craft landed in New Mexico.
   c. An alien was kidnapped by U.S. Air Force pilots.

2. **Native Americans in Canada used to throw something in the water to keep Ogopogo from eating them. What was it?**
   a. seagrass
   b. meat
   c. wild rice

3. **Which ancient people created the best-known mummies *ever*?**
   a. the Greeks
   b. the Egyptians
   c. the Cro-Magnons

4. Some scientists believe that Nessie is this kind of dinosaur:

a. plesiosaur

b. hadrosaur

c. scotsosaur

5. Where was the famous mummy Juanita found?

a. Mexico

b. Canada

c. Peru

6. Which of the following is an actual, enormous sea creature?

a. oarfish

b. soarfish

c. rowfish

7. The most famous picture ever taken of Nessie is called:

a. the Monster's Photo

b. the Scientist's Photo

c. the Surgeon's Photo

8. What body part was NOT visible on the Roswell aliens?

a. hands

b. eyes

c. ears

9. **What is the name of the bone at the base of your tongue that helps you speak?**
   a. the hyoid bone
   b. the humerus bone
   c. the loquacious bone

10. **What type of being eventually overtook the Neandertals?**
    a. *Homo erectus*
    b. *Homo sapiens*
    c. Cro-Magnon

Answers to Bizarre Beings: The Ultimate Challenge

10. c	9. a
8. c	7. c
6. a	5. c
4. a	3. b
2. b	1. b

GROSS-OUT GLOSSARY

Abduct; abduction (ub-DUKT; ub-DUK-shun): to move someone without their consent; the act of moving someone without their consent.

A.C.E.: initials that stand for After the Common Era, a way to identify the date of things that are less than about 2,000 years old.

Anthropologist (ann-throw-POHL-oh-jist): a scientist who studies humans.

Archaeologist (ar-kee-ohl-oh-jist): a scientist who studies artifacts, fossils, and other materials from the past.

Artifact (AR-tih-fact): an object that is left behind by people who lived in the past.

B.C.E.: initials that stand for Before the Common Era, a way to identify things that are more than about 2,000 years old.

Decomposition (dee-comp-o-ZI-shun): the process by which organic matter breaks down after death.

Fossil (fah-sil): hardened remain or trace of an animal or plant from a previous geological period, preserved in rock form on the earth's crust.

Tannic acid (TAN-ik AS-id): a dark-brown, staining acid producing by peat bogs. Also found in tea.